Phonics Fun
Reading Program Book 9: b

W9-CFC-375

At
Bat

by Grace Maccarone

Illustrated by Tom Lapadula

Based on the books by Norman Bridwell

SCHOLASTIC INC.
New York Toronto London Auckland Sydney
Mexico City New Delhi Hong Kong Buenos Aires

I bat the ball.
See it go!

T-Bone has it.
Good catch!

Mom bats the ball.
See it go!

Mac has it.
Good catch!

Dad bats the ball.
See it go!

See the ball go, go, go!

Clifford stops the ball.

Cleo has it!
What fun!

"I knew it! Someone forgot to pay! That was exactly what I was going to say next!" said SpongeBob.

"That is what I have been trying to tell you," said Squidward. "It was only a small mistake, not one of your tall tales."

"Sorry, I forgot to pay my bill," said the customer. "No trouble at all," said Mr. Krabs. "No trouble at all."

"Or a scary coin-eating monster with big jaws?" called SpongeBob. "Who can gnaw through walls!"

"No, that is not it at all," said Squidward.

"I know," called SpongeBob.
"How about an outlaw?
 A tall, mean, coin-grabbing,
 straw-stealing outlaw."
"No, that is not it at all,"
 said Squidward.

"Maybe it was Plankton," said SpongeBob. "He always does awful things!"

"No, that is not it at all," said Squidward.

Later, Mr. Krabs saw that some money was missing from the drawer. "My coins are not all here!" he called.